Special thanks to Venetia Davie, Ryan Ferguson, Sarah Lazar, Charnita Belcher, Tanya Mann, Julia Phelps, Nicole Corse, Sharon Woloszyk, Rita Lichtwardt, Carla Alford, Rob Hudnut, David Wiebe, Shelley Dvi-Vardhana, Gabrielle Miles, Julie Osborn, Rainmaker Entertainment, and Patricia Atchison and Zeke Norton

Published in the United States by Random House Children's Books, a division of Random House LLC, 1745 Broadway, New York, NY 10019, and in Canada by Random House of Canada Limited, Toronto, Penguin Random House Companies. Random House and the colophon are registered trademarks of Random House LLC.

ISBN 978-0-553-50888-8 (trade)
ISBN 978-0-375-97472-4 (lib. bdg.)
ISBN 978-0-553-50889-5 (ebook)
randomhousekids.com
Printed in the United States of America
10 9 8 7 6 5 4 3 2 1   First Edition

Adapted by Molly McGuire Woods

Based on the original screenplay by Marsha Griffin

Illustrated by Ulkutay Design Group

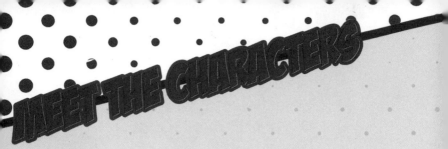

MEET THE CHARACTERS

BARON VON RAVENDALE: KING KRISTOFF'S TRUSTED ADVISOR. HE SECRETLY WANTS TO TAKE OVER THE THRONE AND CREATES A SUPERPOWER POTION TO DO SO.

BRUCE: BARON VON RAVENDALE'S FROG SIDEKICK.

CORINNE: PRINCESS KARA'S COUSIN. SHE IS JEALOUS OF KARA AND DREAMS OF BEING A PRINCESS, TOO.

DARK SPARKLE: CORINNE'S SUPERHERO ALTER EGO AND SUPER SPARKLE'S BIGGEST RIVAL.

GABBY AND ZOOEY: PRINCESS KARA'S ENERGETIC LITTLE SISTERS.

KING KRISTOFF: PRINCESS KARA'S FATHER, THE KING OF WINDEMERE.

MADISON AND MAKALYA: PRINCESS KARA'S BEST FRIENDS. THEY'RE EXTREMELY SMART TWINS WHO INVENT NEW GADGETS FOR PRINCESS KARA—AND SUPER SPARKLE!

NEWTON AND PARKER: NEWTON IS PRINCESS KARA'S ADORABLE PUPPY, AND PARKER IS HER SISTERS' CUDDLY KITTEN.

PRINCESS KARA: THE PRINCESS OF WINDEMERE. SHE WANTS TO MAKE A DIFFERENCE IN HER KINGDOM BUT ISN'T SURE HOW—ESPECIALLY WHEN HER PARENTS ARE SO OVERPROTECTIVE.

QUEEN KARINA: PRINCESS KARA'S MOTHER, THE QUEEN OF WINDEMERE,

SUPER SPARKLE: PRINCESS KARA'S SUPER POWERFUL SUPERHERO ALTER EGO. SHE HAS A SECRET LAIR IN PRINCESS KARA'S BEDROOM.

WES RIVERS: A REPORTER WHO BLOGS ABOUT SUPER SPARKLE.

"This is your best invention!" Princess

Kara shouted to her best friends, Madison

and Makalya. Kara was zooming through

the sky in a flying machine. She could see

the whole kingdom. Windemere looked

so small! She watched her parents, the

king and queen, drive through the front

gate. They were probably returning from

somewhere exciting. Kara wished she

could go somewhere exciting. But her parents always said it was too dangerous.

Down below, Madison and Makalya followed Kara on their power scooters.

They were super smart twins. They invented cool gadgets for Kara to try. Kara's puppy, Newton, and her sisters' kitten, Parker, rode along, too.

"I found the perfect spot for my community garden!" Princess Kara called. She pointed to a spot below. Then she lost control of the flying machine and crashed into a tree!

Her parents rushed over to make sure

she was okay. They were always worrying about her.

"I'm fine," Kara said. "Next time I will be more careful."

"There will be no next time. The world is more dangerous than you realize," said the king. He turned to his royal advisor. "Don't you agree, Baron Von Ravendale?"

The baron nodded. "Without question, Your Majesty. These are troubling times indeed."

"*Ribbit!*" agreed his sidekick, a frog named Bruce.

Kara frowned. Being a princess was

so boring! Kara wanted to do something *important*. If only she could make her parents understand.

In the royal garden that afternoon, Kara and the twins had a tea party. Kara's little sisters, Gabby and Zooey, joined them. So did Kara's cousin Corinne, who was visiting for the summer. She thought Kara's life was perfect and was jealous that Kara was a princess.

A sparkling butterfly fluttered by the table. Corinne waved it away, and it landed on Kara's forehead. It kissed her lightly and then flew away.

That was strange, Kara thought. She
had never seen a butterfly sparkle before.

She started to feel dizzy. "I feel kind of weird," she said. Kara's friends and family rushed to her side just as she fainted.

Kara awoke the next day. She was safe in her bed. She felt much better. She heard mewing outside. Parker was stuck in a nearby tree.

"It's okay. I'll get you," Kara said. She stepped onto the windowsill and reached for the scared kitten. She couldn't reach her. She stretched and stretched. "Gotcha!" she said. Then she looked down. Her feet

were no longer on the windowsill. She was flying!

Kara was frantic. She flapped her arms and swam through the air. A trail of magical sparkles drifted behind her. Kara's mind raced. How was this happening? She looked down and spotted the twins.

"Whoa!" the girls cried in surprise. They raced to Kara's room.

"Any idea what's happening to me?" Kara asked.

"Do you have other superpowers?" Makalya asked. "Like superstrength?"

Kara wasn't sure. She tried to lift her bed. No problem. Superstrength—check.

"Agility?"

Kara tried to scale the wall. Easy! Superagility—check.

"Anything else?" Makalya asked.

Kara raised her hands. Pink sparkles shot from her fingers!

Madison crossed her arms. "Yup. You're a superhero," she announced.

Makalya nodded. "You've got Princess Power!"

"But how?" Kara asked. Then she remembered the sparkling butterfly that had kissed her cheek. Suddenly it all made sense. "That's it!" she cried. "I got kissed by a magical bug, and now I have superpowers." She flew into the air and grinned at the twins. "Are you guys

thinking what I'm thinking?"

"Test drive!" the twins cried. They raced to get their scooters.

Kara zoomed through the sky, testing her new skills. She used her sparkle

powers to make cloud tunnels to race through. She flew into a nearby volcano and picked a flower. She was having such a great time she didn't notice the tree right in front of her. *SMACK!* She crashed into it.

Kara was embarrassed. "This tree has got to go."

Madison shook her head. "That would be against the superhero code of conduct."

Kara paused. "There's a code?"

Makalya nodded. "Powers can only be used to help others."

"We need to find you a mission,"

Madison said. Makalya agreed with her.

Kara thought for a moment. "How about the community garden?"

The twins thought it was perfect. The community garden would definitely help others. With Kara's powers, they could finish it in a snap!

Then Kara remembered her parents. If they knew about her powers, they would never let her use them. They wanted to protect her from danger.

Madison had an idea. What if Kara had a secret identity? When she needed her superpowers, she could change from a princess into . . . Super Sparkle! Kara would be a secret superhero. She could use her powers for good, and no one would know it was her!

Super Sparkle needed just one thing: a super secret disguise!

3

A little while later, Kara stepped out of her dressing room. Madison and Makalya had made her a shimmering gown with a wide belt around the waist.

Kara pushed a button on the belt and her dress turned into a body suit with pink boots, a pink cape, and a sparkling pink mask. She was Super Sparkle!

As she flew to the garden, Super Sparkle noticed some trouble in the city below. A crane was out of control at a construction site! It was knocking steel beams everywhere. Super Sparkle saw Corinne walking nearby. A beam was headed right for her!

Super Sparkle had to help! She raced toward the construction site. She used her superstrength to stop the beam from falling on Corinne.

Then Super Sparkle saw a man snapping pictures of the accident. It was Wes Rivers. He ran Windemere's biggest news website. He was famous for getting to the bottom of stories. Super Sparkle stopped a beam from landing on him, too.

Wes looked shocked. "Thank you!" he said.

"My pleasure," Super Sparkle replied.

Wes snapped a picture of her.

Super Sparkle hardly noticed. She was busy waving at the crowd. As a princess, she was used to attention. But being a superhero was different. It felt amazing to actually *help* people!

Then her cell phone beeped. She checked it. "Oh no! I forgot about the royal reception!"

Super Sparkle raced through the castle hallways. She checked herself in a mirror. *Yikes!* She'd forgotten to change back into Princess Kara. She pushed the button on her belt. Her superhero outfit became her princess dress. She hurried to her bedroom to meet the twins.

"We waited for you at the community garden. But you never showed up," Makalya said.

Kara explained about the construction site. "It got me thinking about all the things I could do with my powers."

"We're one step ahead of you!" Makalya said.

Madison whipped out a remote control and pushed a button. Kara watched her room turn into a secret superhero hideout! Her mirror even changed into a computer screen.

Just then, an emergency alarm sounded.

"Looks like we have our first mission!" Madison said.

"It's Super Sparkle time!" the girls exclaimed.

Over the next few days, Super Sparkle was so busy helping people that she hardly had time to breathe. She stopped thieves and put out fires. She also kept her identity a secret.

Super Sparkle wasn't the only one working hard. Wes Rivers posted tons of stories about Super Sparkle on his website. Everyone in the kingdom wanted

to know who Super Sparkle was.

Even Kara's little sisters had Super Sparkle fever. They wore pink superhero costumes around the castle!

Before Kara knew it, her birthday arrived. The twins gave her a gift. It was a beautiful, sparkling ring! But it wasn't *just* a ring.

"It has a holographic screen, crystals, and a mini lip gloss!" Makalya said. She explained all the ways the ring would help Super Sparkle on her missions.

Kara hugged the twins. She felt lucky to have such awesome friends.

The royal family was throwing Kara a big birthday party. The press arrived to cover the event. But the reporters only wanted to talk about Super Sparkle!

"Has the royal family met Super Sparkle?" Wes Rivers asked.

The queen shook her head. "But the king and I are very grateful for her."

"Windemere is lucky to have such a hero," the king added.

Kara hid a smile. It felt wonderful to have her parents so proud of her—even if they didn't know it!

Then Kara's ring beeped.

"We'll cover for you," Madison said.

Kara snuck out of the room. Time to sparkle!

On her ring screen, Kara saw a man stuck on the side of a mountain. A huge rock was rolling down toward him.

Super Sparkle arrived just in time. She used her superstrength to stop the rock. Then she rescued the man.

"Baron Von Ravendale?" she said when she saw him. What was her father's advisor doing on the side of a mountain?

Super Sparkle didn't have time to worry

about it. She hoped he wouldn't recognize

her.

Just then, Super Sparkle spotted

something purple and shiny flying toward
her. It was another superhero! She was
dressed just like Super Sparkle, but in
purple and blue.

"Out of my way! Dark Sparkle's got this!" the purple hero said. She bumped into Super Sparkle.

Super Sparkle was shocked! Who was Dark Sparkle? What did she want? And why did she look so familiar?

Dark Sparkle zoomed toward the crumbling mountain. She shot purple magic blasts at the falling rocks. Dark Sparkle was trying to help, but she wasn't very good at using her powers. Instead of stopping the rocks, she caused an avalanche!

Super Sparkle looked at the road below.

If she didn't stop those rocks, Windemere would be crushed! She smashed the rocks and saved the day.

Dark Sparkle stomped her foot in midair. She was mad that Super Sparkle had gotten in her way. She flew off in a huff.

Back at headquarters, Kara told the twins about Dark Sparkle. "She is a total rookie!"

"There's room in the kingdom for more than one hero, right?" Makalya said.

Kara frowned. It was exciting being the only hero in town. She didn't want to share the spotlight with Dark Sparkle. But it looked like she had no choice.

Over the next few days, every time Super Sparkle arrived to help, Dark Sparkle did, too. They got in each other's way. Kara was so frustrated!

One day, Dark Sparkle beat Super Sparkle to a rescue. Dark Sparkle was a hero! She landed on the front page of Wes Rivers's website.

Kara fumed. Everywhere she went, people only talked about Dark Sparkle. Even her little sisters dressed in purple now. Things could not get any worse. But then she checked Wes Rivers's website.

At the top of the page, the headline read: "Princess Superhero!" Wes Rivers had figured out that she was Super Sparkle! Now the whole kingdom would know. Her parents would find out! Kara groaned. This was definitely worse.

At dinner, Kara's parents ordered her to stop being Super Sparkle.

"While you live under our roof, you are not to act as Super Sparkle," the queen said.

"That is final," added the king.

Kara hung her head.

Across the table, Corinne spoke. "On the bright side, the kingdom still has

Dark Sparkle. I'm sure she can handle whatever comes up."

Just then, the dining room doors crashed open. Baron Von Ravendale flew into the room with Bruce. The baron had invented a potion to give himself evil powers. He wanted the kingdom for himself! He planned to destroy the royal family.

Now it makes sense, Kara thought. The baron had been on the mountain collecting ingredients for his potion! Kara was sure he was also behind the sparkle butterfly that had given her superpowers.

The baron raised his hands. He shot dark green evil orbs toward the table.

The royal family dove for cover.

Suddenly, Corinne shot a blast of purple magic from her hands.

Kara's jaw dropped. Purple magic? "You're Dark Sparkle?" she cried.

Corinne nodded. Then she pushed Kara out of the way.

Kara pushed back. Super Sparkle and Dark Sparkle would *not* be working together anytime soon!

Kara turned into Super Sparkle. She quickly took her family to the kingdom's

safety tower. Dark Sparkle stayed behind
to battle with Baron Von Ravendale.

Super Sparkle hugged her parents
goodbye and raced back to the ballroom.

She crashed into Dark Sparkle.

"Where's the baron?" Super Sparkle asked.

"I lost him," Dark Sparkle replied.

"Just stay back, okay?" Super Sparkle said. "I don't want your help."

Dark Sparkle crossed her arms. "You're not the boss! You never let anybody else share the spotlight, not even for a second."

"Get your own life, Corinne!" Super Sparkle shouted. "No matter how bad you want it, you can't have mine!"

"You think you can do it alone?" Dark Sparkle asked, sounding hurt. "Be my guest!" She zoomed out of the room, leaving Super Sparkle on her own.

A few minutes later, Super Sparkle found the baron trying to break into the tower!

He shot a sparkle orb at her, but she dodged it. Then she shot a glittering ball of magic at him. It knocked him to the ground.

But the baron wasn't finished. "There's more than one way to destroy a king," he growled. He sped toward the volcano. He was going to make it erupt and destroy the kingdom!

Super Sparkle followed him.

The baron fired bolts of magic at the volcano. The volcano rumbled. Steam rose from its opening. Lava started to bubble over.

Super Sparkle tried to stop the lava. It was rising too quickly! She needed another plan. Maybe she could trap the lava inside the volcano. Super Sparkle shot magic orbs toward the volcano's mouth. She needed help. It wasn't working!

The lava escaped. It flowed right toward the castle—and the royal family!

The lava surrounded the tower. The royal family was trapped! The tower started to break away from the castle. Super Sparkle braced it with her superstrength. The royal family was safe—for now. But Super Sparkle needed a way to change the lava's path. If she could make it flow *around* the city, they would all be safe. She started to blast a new path for the lava. But it was coming too fast!

Then she saw a purple blur in the sky.

"Corinne?" she cried. Dark Sparkle landed next to her. She shot her sparkling orbs and helped blast new paths, too.

"I may have a lot of faults. And I am not your biggest fan," Dark Sparkle said. "But you'd never walk away from something like this, and neither can I!"

Super Sparkle nodded. They needed to put aside their differences and work together to save the kingdom.

Using their sparkling magic, the two superheroes changed the lava's path.

"We did it!" Super Sparkle exclaimed.

"Not bad for two people who kept

getting in each other's way." Dark Sparkle replied.

"I'm sorry I was so harsh before," Super Sparkle said.

Dark Sparkle shook her head. "No, I've always wanted your life. It just seemed better to be *you*."

"Trust me, it isn't," Super Sparkle said. "Not when you consider the way I've been acting lately."

A huge blast exploded nearby! Baron Von Ravendale was shooting evil orbs at them!

The girls shot sparkle-charged orbs back at the baron.

"Hey, Baron," Dark Sparkle called. "Didn't anybody ever tell you—"

"Two is *always* better than one!" Super Sparkle finished. She high-fived her cousin.

Then Bruce shot through the sky. He had superpowers, too! He tried to use his

long frog tongue to tie the girls together.
But Parker and Newton flew out of
nowhere and stopped him. Super Sparkle
couldn't believe her eyes. How had the
pets gained superpowers? She could only

guess that the sparkling butterfly was behind that, too.

Working together, Super Sparkle and Dark Sparkle defeated the baron. Parker and Newton handled Bruce. The royal family left the tower, and the superheroes locked the baron and Bruce inside.

The royal family rushed toward the girls.

"Dark Sparkle! Can I be you when I grow up?" Gabby asked.

Dark Sparkle laughed. "I think it'd be much cooler to be yourself." She winked at Super Sparkle.

The king said, "You proved yourself and took care of us. For that we are proud . . . of both of you."

Super Sparkle grinned. "Thanks, Dad. You were right. Things weren't as safe around here as I thought." She glanced at her cousin. "But now the kingdom has *two* superheroes watching its back!"

Woof! Meow! Sparkle Pup and Kitty Sparkle called as they jumped up and down.

"Make that four!" Super Sparkle said, giggling. She smiled at Dark Sparkle. "I lost track of why I wanted to make a difference in the first place."

"To make Windemere a better place," Dark Sparkle replied.

Super Sparkle nodded. "Speaking of that, don't we have a job to do?"

She led the group to the community garden. They got to work planting seeds.

Wes Rivers was there, taking pictures as usual. "It's called a *community* garden, Wes," Kara called. "Grab a shovel!"

"This is payback for blowing your cover, isn't it?" Wes asked.

"Totally!" Kara winked. She looked around at her family and friends. They were working together for the good of Windemere. Kara realized that she didn't need superpowers at all. She had something better: the power of friendship. And nothing sparkled brighter than that.